A Love Letter To Jamaica.

Michael Brigden

A Love Letter To Jamaica

Copyright © 2023 Michael Paul Brigden

All rights reserved.

ISBN: **9798388403100**

DEDICATION

I not only dedicate this book to my wife Teshea, my family and friends in Jamaica but also the island itself. You are my inspiration, my muse and fascination. I fell for you long ago and my love affair continues on.

A Love Letter To Jamaica

A Love Letter To Jamaica

CONTENTS

	Acknowledgments	i
1	First Time	Pg 2
2	No Worry	Pg 4
3	On Offer	Pg 6
4	Wonders	Pg 8
5	The Couple	Pg 10
6	Honest talk	Pg 12
7	It Likkle But It Tallowah	Pg 14
8	When I Fell In Love With An Island	Pg 16
9	Resolve	Pg 18
10	Best Friends	Pg 20
11	When We First Met	Pg 22
12	Out Of Many	Pg 24
13	A Love Affair	Pg 26
14	Broken Backs	Pg 28
15	History	Pg 30
16	There is a Rhythm	Pg 32
17	Faith's Pen	Pg 34
18	Jamaica	Pg 36
19	Northern Shores	Pg 38
20	Little Ochie	Pg 40

21	The Fruit That Grows and Grows	Pg 42
22	Place After Place	Pg 44
23	Dunn's River	Pg 46
24	Bamboo Grove	Pg 48
25	I Remember	Pg 50
26	The Mighty Guinep	Pg 52
27	New Tastes	Pg 54
28	Jamaica 2	Pg 56
29	History	Pg 58
30	Second Home	Pg 60
31	One	Pg 62
32	It May Be Likkle	Pg 64
33	Temptation	Pg 66
34	Salt River	Pg 68
35	Virgin Sands	Pg 70
36	May Pen	Pg 72
37	Your Charm	Pg 74
38	We Likkle But We Tallowah	Pg 76
39	In A Split Second I Am With You	Pg 78
40	Lloyd	Pg 80

A Love Letter To Jamaica

ACKNOWLEDGMENTS

I have to start by thanking my wife for reading through the many poems you see in the pages that follow, giving her thoughts and support throughout the writing of this book. Her insights and constructive advice have been extremely helpful and have hopefully helped me capture the beauty I feel in my heart. I would also like to thank family and friends in Jamaica who by their continued warmth inspire me to capture this vibrancy and passion in my words. Lastly I have to mention the island itself, Jamaica, you have become my muse, my fascination and my love.

A Love Letter To Jamaica

A Love Letter To Jamaica

FIRST TIME

The first time that I met you
as we touched down on your land,
the sound rang out inside the plane
with the coming together of hands,
the applause aimed at the pilot
and the fact we had set down
safely in this cherished place
and this act I found profound,
I'd never heard of this before
or witnessed it take place,
I guess I should have found it odd
but it felt a bit like grace,
a thank you to the pilot
and to our God above
to safely bring us to the place
that I would grow to love.

© The Ordinary Poet

A Love Letter To Jamaica

NO WORRY

You've shown me wonders,
you've fed me well,
you've given friendship
of which I tell
to all who'll listen
around the world,
there is this place
where bliss unfurls
and wraps you up
in loving arms,
its nature slow,
it's peace and calm
transferred to people
who cannot rush,
they'll take their time
not speed and push
and they'll soon come
but in their time,
just settle back
it's paradigm.

© The Ordinary Poet

ON OFFER

A land that has a lot to offer
yet more there's under wraps,
more to tantalise the senses
than tourists often trap,
a sense of something round the corner
that darting eyes might miss,
a little peace of heaven given
that provides a lifetime's bliss,
a little piece of history
that beggars questions of
what and where and when and how
to understand the love
of just how rich this fertile land is
and what the land's been through,
so much hidden in plain sight
if one only knew.

© The Ordinary Poet

WONDERS

I've seen a sky kaleidoscopic
as light breaks through the clouds,
the final dregs of sunshine beams
before the night's long shroud,
I've been amazed as lightening strikes
split up across the sky
and roads are running like flooded rivers,
or deserted and bone dry,
I've seen the sky a fiery red
as though it were aflame,
all of these took me to rest
at peace and stresses tamed.

© The Ordinary Poet

THE COUPLE

Wrinkle hands hold wrinkled hands,
both walking side by side,
ancient love sprung from the day
this man walked with his bride,
the care apparent for all to see
in an act of lifelong love,
two lovers born in different times
still fit like hand in glove.

© The Ordinary Poet

A Love Letter To Jamaica

HONEST TALK

Everything is everything
and all is all you'll see,
straight talking is a part of life
and the only way to be,
no flowering up a story
when the plain truth should be told,
it's honesty but said with care
that outsiders see as bold
or even worse as rudeness
but you see it's what it is,
honest folk with honest talk
that outsiders often miss.

© The Ordinary Poet

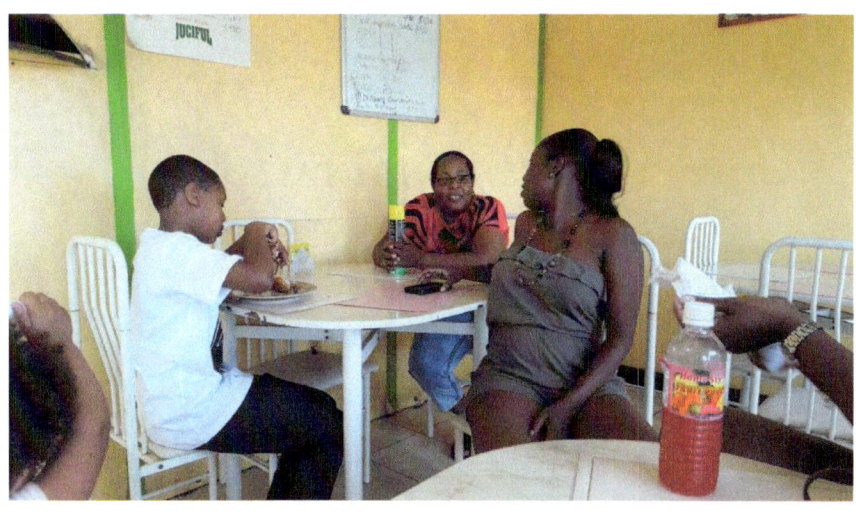

IT LIKKLE BUT IT TALLOWAH

A past that must not be forgotten
as they forge into the new,
embracing all these many cultures,
for the many not the few,
to show the world another face
of what a place can be
when all within society
are equal and are free,
a land that has a lot to say
and so much more to give
it may be little in its size
but it's presence mighty big.

© The Ordinary Poet

A Love Letter To Jamaica

WHEN I FELL IN LOVE WITH AN ISLAND

You gave me smiles
and miles and miles
of good vibrations,
sweet loving arms
like balm to calm
my weary bones.

You offered peace
caprice that would not cease
ad infinitum,
a place called home
to comb and roam
throughout my days.

You made me free
to be and justly see
the world around me,
your bounty weighed
your grade conveyed
to all who see.

© The Ordinary Poet

A Love Letter To Jamaica

A Love Letter To Jamaica

RESOLVE

In some there's a hardship written in lines across hardened faces
entrenched and ingrained,
centuries of evil marked out on skin,
that relay their troubles and shows off their pain
and yet there's resolve and a strength in their stride,
that nothing can harm or the future deny
as they push through their days with a hard battled smile,
a picture of fortitude through each daily trial,
then back to their homesteads, their shacks and their yaads
for a moment of comfort with kin,
the clicking of tiles and of glass and of doors
take them to their bed till the new day begins.

© The Ordinary Poet

BEST FRIENDS

We are like long lost friends,
we meet and greet
as though we met just yesterday
and yet the years have passed.

We hardly talk when we're apart,
we meet and greet
as though the miles disolve away,
such feelings we've amassed.

We are but just a moment from
we meet and greet
with no need for words of love,
for our friendship shared holds fast.

We part as though the days flew by
we meet and greet
and say goodbye
but know this time won't last.

© The Ordinary Poet

WHEN FIRST WE MET

I first saw in August,
you were hot
and I warmed to you,
I was made to feel welcome,
so very welcome,
like I had finally found home.

You caressed my senses
with sights and sounds
that I had not known before,
something new
and yet an ancient feel,
like I had finally found home.

Days became weeks
as I fell for you,
a love had blossomed
and grown in my heart,
a passion I could not fight,
like I had finally found home.

The first time I left you
I cried,
each time since
has been the same,
I mourn a lost love
like I have left my home.

© The Ordinary Poe

OUT OF MANY

Out of many,
they unite,
many came
together light,
a varied people,
who live as one,
from shore to shore,
a land they won,
from coast to coast,
from yaad to steeple
out of many
they are one people.

© The Ordinary Poet

A LOVE AFFAIR

With you I have a love affair,
a passion for your feel,
my every sense revitalized,
your true self is revealed,
I long to be within your shores
and feel your spirit rise
and comfort me with reverence,
the greatest of all highs,
I sense you coursing through my blood
I hear this beat inside,
getting stronger till the day
when I'll be by your side,
farewell is not goodbye for good,
it is only till then
when as lovers we will meet
and share our hearts again.

© The Ordinary Poet

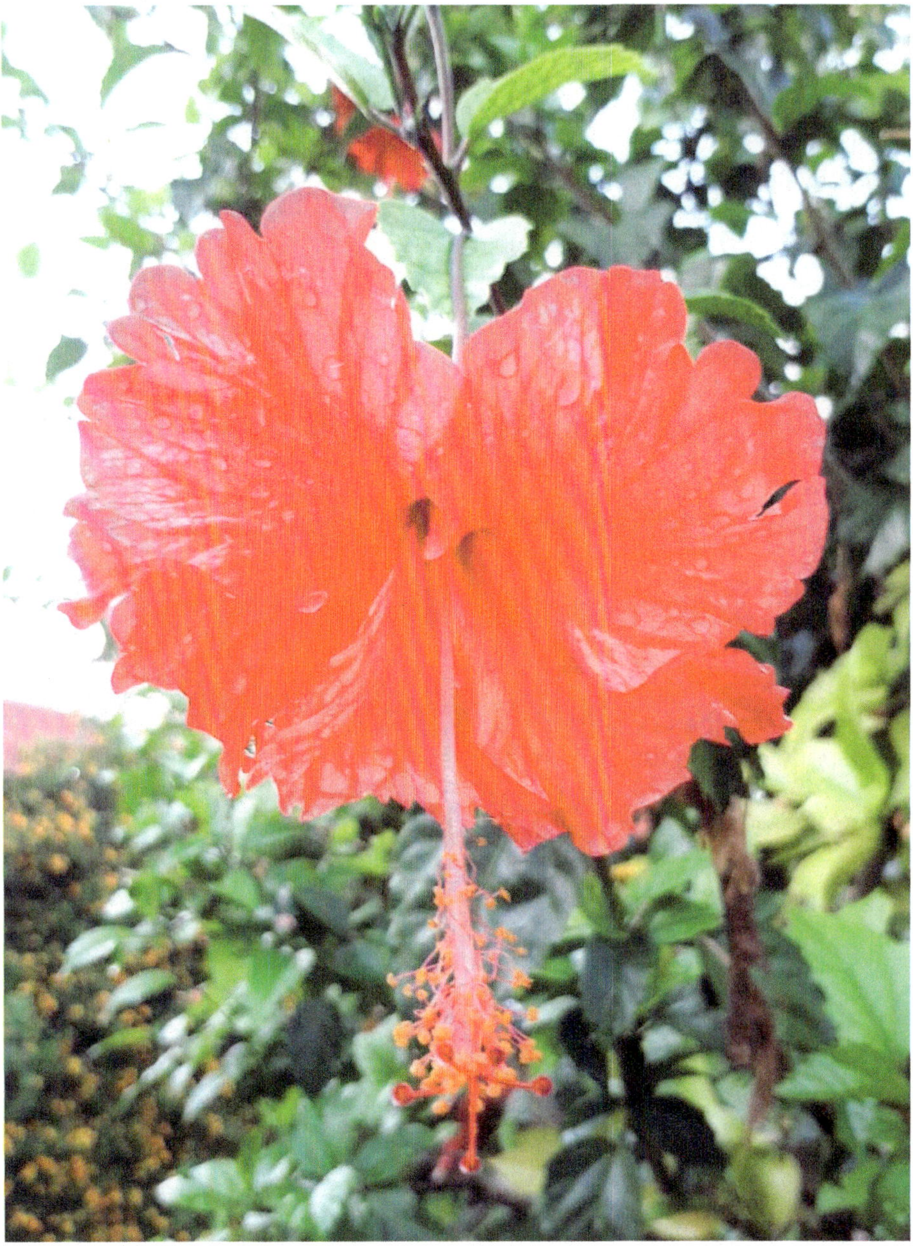

BROKEN BACKS

Names of places
mark a past
that remind us
verse by verse,
when through adversity we toiled
to line the white man's purse.

Such riches built
off broken backs
that cannot
be replaced,
there's no amount of reparation
can wipe tears from their face.

A strength exists
within the people
to keep the
names alive,
reminders of these deadly times,
when it was hard just to survive.

© The Ordinary Poet

A Love Letter To Jamaica

HISTORY

There is a pride
that you can feel
within their hearts that all have won,
so brazen,
worn upon their chests,
this land of many,
joined as one.

There is a sense
of more to come
out of this land of green and gold,
a hope,
a notion of a time,
when all is good
within their fold.

There is a knowledge
of a past,
of a rich and royal time,
a history,
of distant lands,
a touch of the sublime.

© The Ordinary Poet

A Love Letter To Jamaica

THERE IS A RHYTHM

A place where even time slows down
and endless sun goes round and round
and dancehall hangs upon the air
with reggae beats that mean to dare
the passer-by to move their feet
and tap along to reggae's beat,
with voices just above a hum
as toes will tap and fingers drum,
a feeling deep within the bones
that we are one and not alone.

© The Ordinary Poet

A Love Letter To Jamaica

FAITH'S PEN

Before new road
mash it up,
there was a place
we used to stop,
for quick refreshment,
a bite to eat,
no trip to Ochi
would be complete
without a stop
at old Faith's Pen,
the smell, the taste,
ten out of ten
and when our bellies
were fit to bust,
a likkle bigger,
our belts adjust
and on our way
upon the road,
off to wherever
was our abode.

© The Ordinary Poet

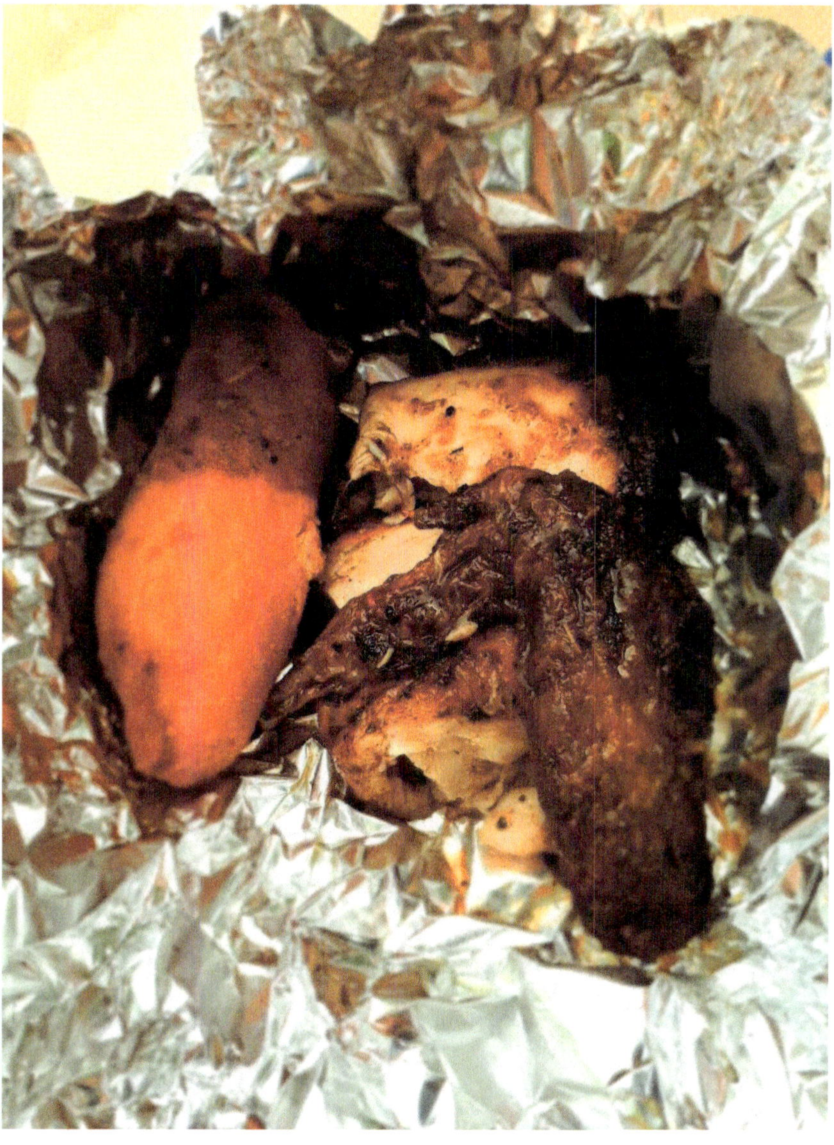

JAMAICA

You haunt me like a lover's kiss,
I miss you like a friend
but just as friendships know no miles
our love will never end,
I see you when I close my eyes,
I feel yellow, green and black
sitting in this heart of mine
that waits till I come back,
your vibrancy leaves marks upon me,
that stay whilst we're apart,
until we meet again my love
I'll keep you in my heart.

© The Ordinary Poet

A Love Letter To Jamaica

NORTHERN SHORES

We walk as two as the sun goes down
and sets below the sea,
we feel the sand between our toes,
you're looking back at me,
I catch reflections in your eyes
of twinkling stars and palms
that hold me like a lullaby
as I lay in your arms,
this could be any stretch of beach
along the northern shores,
miles and miles of unspoilt sand,
how could we want for more,
we sit until the hours grow short
and the sun begins to rise,
not a single word was spoken
as love has our tongues tied.

© The Ordinary Poet

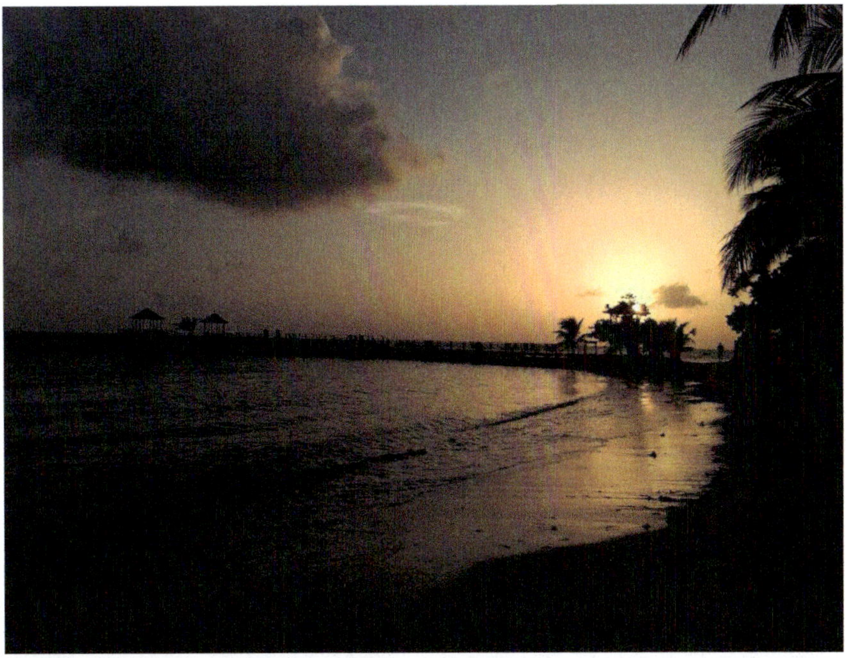

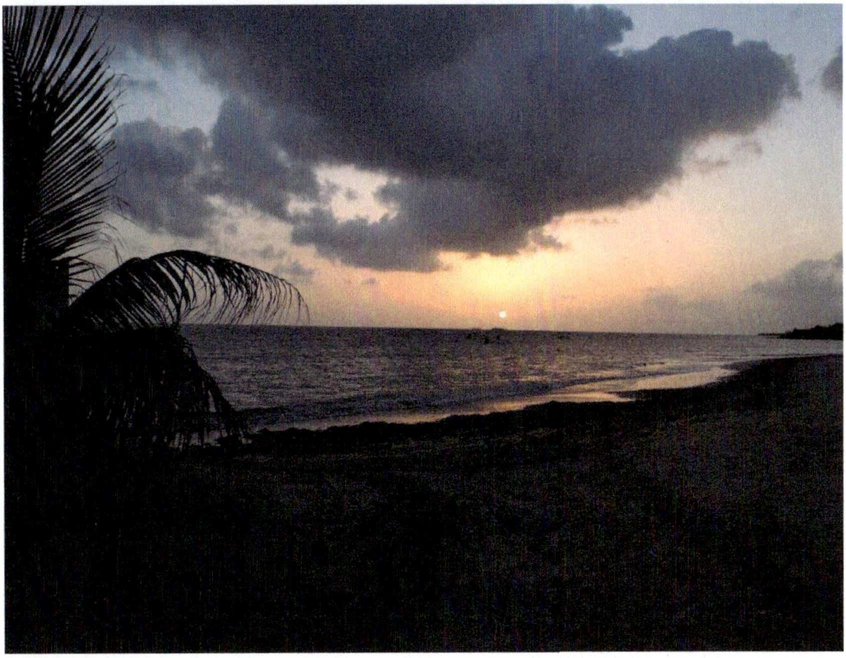

LITTLE OCHIE

There's this place called Little Ochie
that's just past Alligator Pond
that serves the most exquisite seafood
of which I am most fond,
steamed or grilled or BBQ'd
Lobster, fish and crab,
with just a little escovitch,
or jerk maybe we'll have,
served on cling filmed platters
and brought to table side,
sat in rows under sea going boats,
our hunger we can't hide,
tucking in after grace is said
as family we eat,
savouring each and every morsel
for these are mighty treats.

© The Ordinary Poet

A Love Letter To Jamaica

THE FRUIT THAT GROWS AND GROWS

In country, town and villages,
in open fields and yaads,
you'll see so many different fruits
just ripening beside,
so many different type of Mango
from Julie, Keith and green,
Kidney, Graham and Hamilton
East Indian are seen
and many more that could be named
each tasting quite unique,
a literal store beside the road
for hungry hands to reach
and then there's Guinep and Soursop,
Ackee and Almonds sweet,
Naseberry and Star Apple
and Sweetsop to compete
with Breadfruit, plum and Tamarind,
with Carambola too,
Papaya, Pineapple and Rambutan
and Coconuts you'll view,
so fertile is this land you see
and it springs forth its fruit
wherever you'll see a patch of land
these beauties sure will shoot.

© The Ordinary Poet

A Love Letter To Jamaica

PLACE AFTER PLACE

Colours that assault the eyes,
vibrant as the Sun,
people mill around in thousands
they smile as if for fun,
names of towns and roads amaze,
they hint at stories old,
a history of sweet Jamaica
waiting to be told,
little shacks that give off heat
and smells of what's inside,
breakfast, lunch or in-between
a taste of the cook's pride,
roads that have seen better days
and yet they will not change
a slalom course for cars and taxis,
as chassis re-arrange,
brick and concrete broken open
as fruit trees spread their wings,
providing up a harvest promise
that makes a poor heart sing,
all of this seen as you travel
everywhere you go,
colours that assault the eyes,
as through your blood they flow.

© The Ordinary Poet

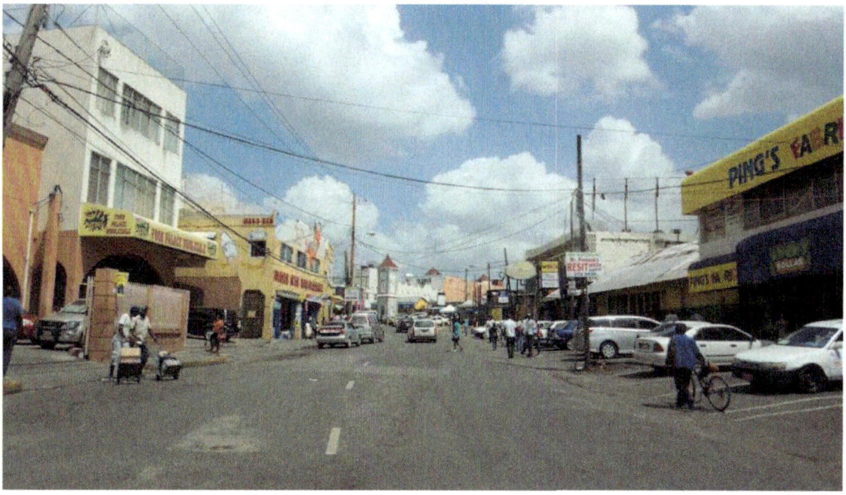
PING'S

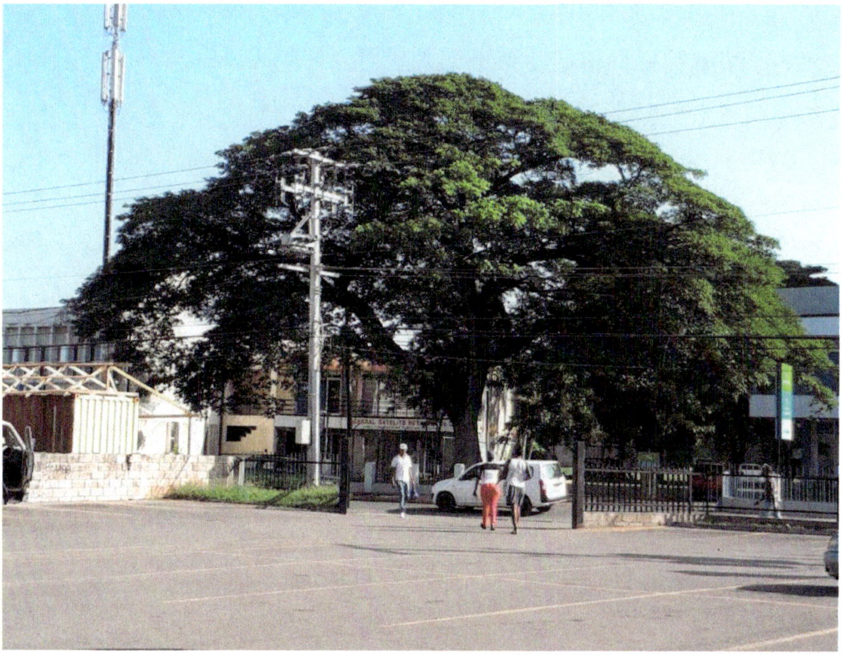

DUNN'S RIVER

There above is power immortal
that thrashes through the rock,
tempting feet to tread with peril
from the bottom to the top,
one after another goes
placing feet precise,
finding purchase through the torrent
that splashes with delight,
the faint will leave as half done
the brave will soldier on,
to stand above this monolith
and feel the day is won.

© The Ordinary Poet

A Love Letter To Jamaica

BAMBOO GROVE

There's a little bit of paradise,
a little treasure trove
as you drive through St Elizabeth,
you'll witness Bamboo Grove,
majestic canes reach to the sky
that curve and joins their ends
forming miles of nature's tunnel
they hug like long lost friends,
your eyes drawn to the magnificence
of shadows cast by the sun,
shining through the majestic canes,
as reality comes undone,
shades of beige and verdent green
blanket either side,
no longer caring where the road goes,
their beauty's not denied,
you long for this to last a lifetime,
this little treasure trove,
found within St Elizabeth,
this place called Bamboo Grove.

© The Ordinary Poet

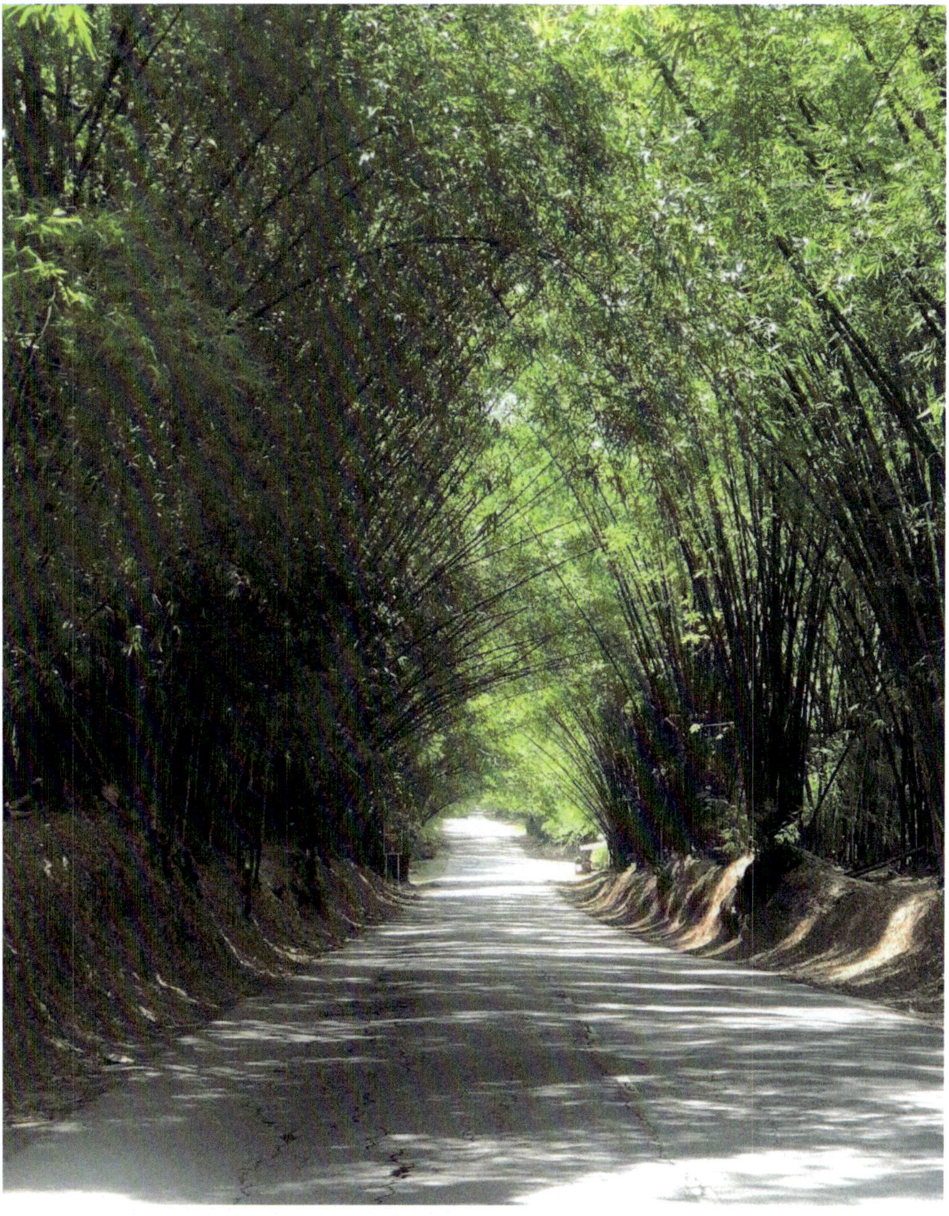

I REMEMBER

I feel the grass beneath my feet,
I see shadows of seats,
Tables,
An altar,
Faces smiling,
An odd tear falling,
As sacred words are spoken,
That unite,
Us as lovers,
Under his gaze,
Forever.

© The Ordinary Poet

A Love Letter To Jamaica

THE MIGHTY GUINEP

There's a fruit that's an enigma,
a true harvest sent from God,
hardly it's an inch across,
to Ambrosia a nod,
it's circular with a green skin
that's cracked between the teeth,
then succulent golden flesh
that's moist and mighty sweet
but then the most amazing thing
where once was taste buds moist,
the mouth becomes an arid place
as more fresh fruit we foist
into a ravenous abyss,
to feed this greed for fruit,
on and on till satisfaction
is met as stomachs mute,
the Guinep offers up surprise
upon surprise and more,
this humble King of all the fruits
is one to be adored.

© The Ordinary Poet

A Love Letter To Jamaica

NEW TASTES

My taste buds
taken on a journey
to the steps of Heaven's gate,
each dish a marvel of desires
and my hunger cannot wait
to try the next sweet recipe
full of fresh abundant wares
spread across this wholesome land
in a place that loves to share,
Curry Goat and Curry Chicken,
Rice and Peas to go,
Mannish Water and Pepper Shrimp,
Ackee and Salt Fish flows,
Brown Stew Chicken and Salt Fish Fritters
Jerk Pork and festival,
Red Pea Soup and Easter Bun,
are just some that I recall,
so many dishes I've discovered
and yet I know there's more
I wonder what I'll next discover,
what's the next that I'll adore.

when I am on your shores.

© The Ordinary Poet

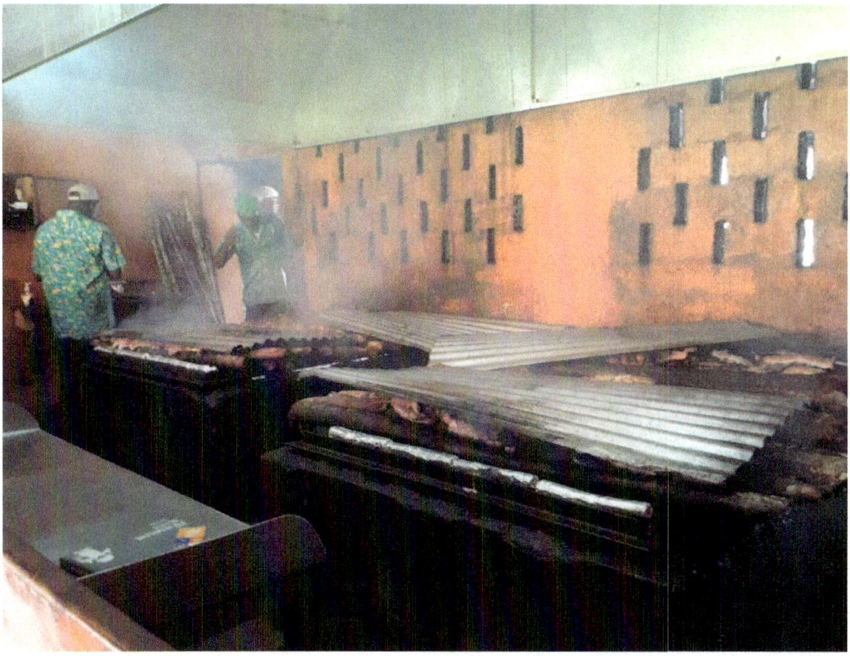

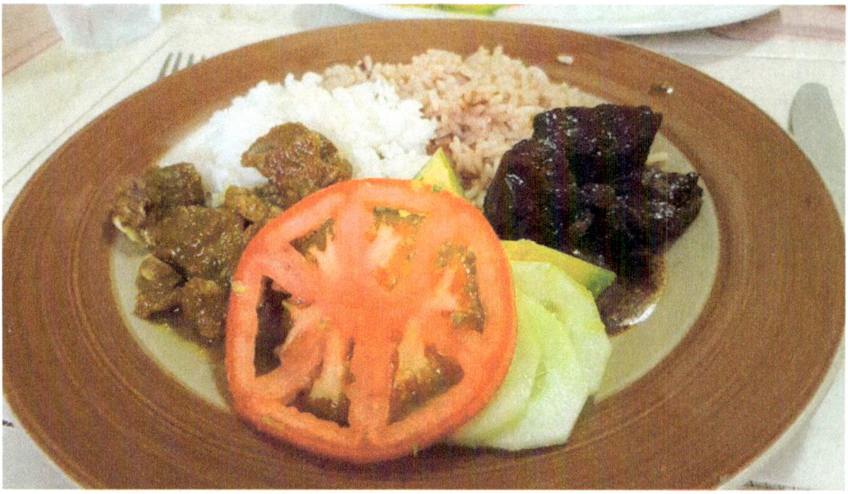

JAMAICA

Your back roads aren't perfect
but they do take you there,
through a green lit by sunshine,
to a sunset to share.

There are colours that are bright
but they're not out of place,
set upon a rich landscape
as history we trace.

The markets are a frenzy,
but there's the sweetest of songs
that hangs in the air,
makes you feel you belong.

There are fruits that seem strange
but this bounty they share,
from hillside to back yard,
they grow everywhere.

The time seems to hold back
but there's moments to think,
to show their desires,
a people in sync.

This Countries an enigma
but it is perfect to me,
a land of one people,
a land of the free.

© The Ordinary Poet

A Love Letter To Jamaica

HISTORY

An evening walk
through history,
a place of peaceful thought
that marks emancipation
with eyes that gaze upon
the heavens in the sky above
in triumph as they rise
from horrors of an evil trade
shown in Redemption Song,
in silence we walked hand in hand
as we cast our minds upon
the meaning of this open space
and the righting of these wrongs.

© The Ordinary Poet

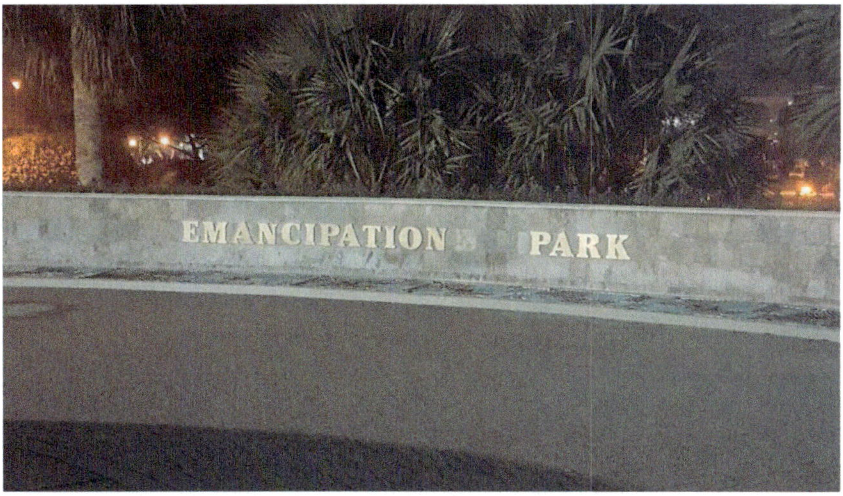
EMANCIPATION PARK

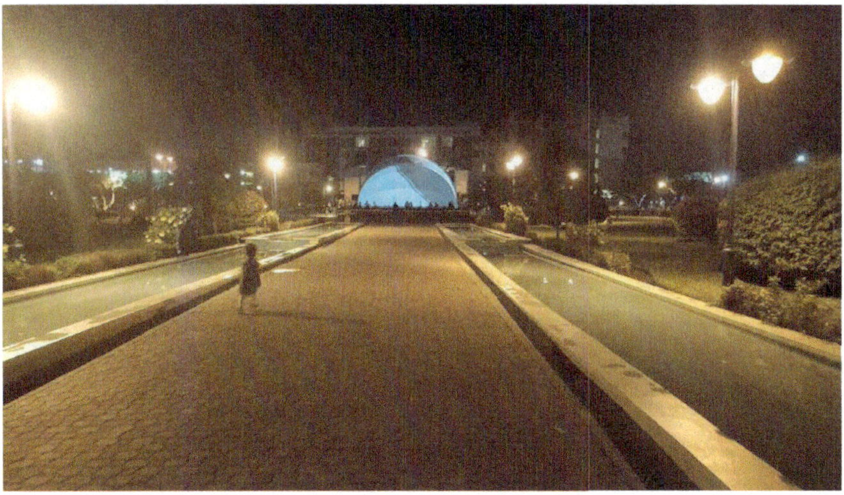

SECOND HOME

You offered me a altar
on which to say my vows,
towards my bride,
to be my wife,
my future life endow,
surrounded by our families
under a sunshine sky,
I spoke of love and tenderness
and promised to my bride
that I would love and care for her
throughout the good and bad
and in response there came the same
how could I be more glad,
the congregation dressed in white
to mark this special day,
underneath Jamaican skies,
this brilliance displayed
then as pronouncement of our state
became a truth for all
we walked under an arch of hands,
no longer two,
a whole,
I remember then we walked together
and spoke as two alone,
a tender moment in a day
when I'd found a second home.

© The Ordinary Poet

A Love Letter To Jamaica

ONE

I feel you under my skin,
Risen desire,
A sheer chord,
Struck,
Between us,
Until me and you,
Unite,
Indistinguishable,
As man and land,
We are now one.

©The Ordinary Poet

A Love Letter To Jamaica

IT MAY BE LIKKLE

I love this land that isn't big,
It likkle but it tallowah,
Out of many came one people,
To this land Jamaica.
It plentiful with food to harvest,
The home of mi sweet Wife,
Jamming to a reggae beat,
This land so full of life.
The black, the green, abundant gold,
To symbolise this land,
The hardship, land and shining Sun,
Make this island grand.
This likkle land has reached out far,
Its effect seen round the world,
The music, athletics, civil rights,
Such pride when flag unfurled.

©The Ordinary Poet

A Love Letter To Jamaica

TEMPTATION

So many foods,
That tempt,
From Bun and Cheese,
To Ackee and Saltfish,
Roasted Breadfruit,
And Manish water,
Steamed Fish
Fried fish,
Escoveitch,
Jerk Chicken and Pork,
And Chicken Foot Soup,
A Jelly,
A Mango straight from the tree,
The tastes of Jamaica,
So tempting to me.

©The Ordinary Poet

A Love Letter To Jamaica

SALT RIVER

Silken waters lightly brackish,
Flows between the trees,
Warmed up by the midday sun,
Cooled down by the breeze.

People gather in the water,
Swimming, having fun,
Children swinging, splashing down,
Under midday Sun.

They say this place has benefits,
This waters minerals,
Making healthy minds and bodies,
Of people one and all.

©The Ordinary Poet

A Love Letter To Jamaica

VIRGIN SANDS

I want to plant my feet,
Upon virgin land,
And you have plenty,
Don't you,
Spreading out,
All around,
Let me walk where no man has tread,
Let mother nature feel me,
Bear my weight,
While I become one,
With the land.

©The Ordinary Poet

A Love Letter To Jamaica

MAY PEN

A late night drive,
Through busy streets,
People still trading,
People still buying,
Car horns are raging,
As traffic competes,
With the life of May Pen.

©The Ordinary Poet

A Love Letter To Jamaica

YOUR CHARM.

I have grown to cherish you,
To see you through a lover's eyes,
The way you reveal yourself,
Your beauty,
Your temperament,
Your style,
You are so much more than first impressions,
Scratch below your surface,
And a hidden charm is there,
Waiting to be discovered,
By a lover's heart.

©The Ordinary Poet

A Love Letter To Jamaica

WE LIKKLE BUT WE TALLAWAH

We are more than one,
Engulfed in Sun.

Land of green and gold,
Incredible views to hold,
Kings and Queens in their yard,
Kings and Queens playing hard,
Loving one, loving all,
Everyone big and small.

Belief in their stature,
Undeniable rapture,
True to their self, their green land their wealth.

Welcome to all,
Everyone hear their call.

The land full of song,
A rhythm so strong,
Like joy to the ears till
Laughter appears,
All over their faces,
With magnificent graces,
And out of this land,
Hail a people real grand.

©The Ordinary Poet

A Love Letter To Jamaica

IN A SPLIT SECOND I AM WITH YOU

I'm transported to a different place
as I think about your land,
I begin to sense the smells and sounds
as my memories they command,
the food cooked by the roadside
or back beat of Reggae
with of course a touch of dancehall
to help me on my way,
then I see the colours
popping through my mist
as memories of places loved
are seen but sorely missed,
the sprawling lush green mountains
and fields of orange groves,
the sound of gushing water
from amazing waterfalls,
all of this in one split second,
a daydream of a place
that I hold so very dear,
a land crammed full of grace.

© The Ordinary Poet

A Love Letter To Jamaica

LLOYD

On the shores of Montego Bay
there's a hotel by the beach,
a bartender who knows my name
and how my thirst to breach,
he goes by the name of Lloyd
and he keeps the poolside bar,
he makes the very best cocktails
of anyone by far,
he makes the time feel special
as we share the moments when
I need a drink to quench my thirst
and we'll talk as long lost friends,
he'll pour my favourite cocktail
a 'Paul Fisher' just for me,
a special drink designed by Lloyd
that's just my cup of tea,
I don't think he knows how special
are the little things he does,
our little shared experience
that's so filled up with love,
I know a little of his life,
he knows a bit of mine,
I treasure all these memories
that I have of my time
spent chatting with this bartender
that I know as my friend Lloyd,
whenever I think of being by the beach,
these memories are deployed.

© The Ordinary Poet

A Love Letter To Jamaica

ABOUT THE AUTHOR

Michael Paul Brigden writes under the pen name 'The Ordinary Poet'. Michael's poems have been published in a variety of journals and anthologies including Songs of Peace (The World's biggest Poetry Anthology 2020), In the Memory of Trayvon Martin (2017), Whispers Journal (2018), Equipoise (Amazon 2018), Poets Pond Volume 2 (Xpress Publishing), Break The Silence (Amazon 2020), Poetica Volume 2 (Amazon 2019), Scarlet Leaf Review (2017), Depression is What Really Killed the Dinosaurs (Amazon 2022), Forget Me Not Press Nothing Gold Can Stay (2022), Hope Is A Group Project (TheWeeSparrowPoetryPress 2022), Querencia Summer Anthology (2022), Magical Midwest-An anthology (2022), Ecological Phsychopoetry (2022/23) and a Commendation in The Stephen Spender Prize 2022. Michael has also self published an anthology of work available on Amazon Living Through Lockdown: The world According To Covid 19 (2020).

Printed in Great Britain
by Amazon